Baby Duckbil

By Beth Spanjian
Illustrated by Karel Havlicek/Novosad

MERRIGOLD PRESS • NEW YORK

Text © 1988 Angel Entertainment, Inc. Illustrations © 1988 Karel Havlicek/Novosad. All rights reserved. First published by Longmeadow Press. Printed in the U.S.A. No part of this book may be reproduced or copied in any form without written permission from the publisher. All trademarks are the property of Merrigold Press, Racine, Wisconsin 53402. Library of Congress Catalog Card Number 90-81289 ISBN 0-307-90901-8   MCMXCIV

The morning sun floods the hillside. Slowly the herd of duck-billed dinosaurs comes to life. Nestled among her brothers and sisters, Baby Duckbill tries to open her eyes.

Mother Duckbill waits patiently at the edge of the nest. She arranges the bedding of plants around her babies, and nudges Baby Duckbill with her huge nose.

Before long, the whole herd is up. Mother Duckbill lowers her muzzle into the nest. She's brought a mouthful of reeds and grasses. Baby Duckbill climbs on top of her brother to reach the food first.

Baby Duckbill and her sister both bite into the same juicy leaf. With one quick jerk, Baby Duckbill pulls the leaf from her sister's mouth, and scrambles across the nest to eat her prize in peace.

A neighboring duckbill passes too close to Baby Duckbill's nest. Mother Duckbill quickly turns toward the dinosaur and roars a warning.

Baby Duckbill and her brothers and sisters have grown large enough to leave their nest. They are now ready to find food for themselves. With a little help from her mother, Baby Duckbill follows her sister out of the nest.

The Duckbill family makes its way through the noisy colony. Mother Duckbill tries to keep her babies close to her side, but Baby Duckbill falls behind, and gets a nip from an unfriendly neighbor.

Baby Duckbill's family joins some other duckbill families quietly eating their fill of plants. Learning from her mother, the little dinosaur nibbles some tender shoots. This time she stays close.

But the forest is filled with dangers, and one
of them soon appears–a hungry tyrannosaurus.
Mother Duckbill lifts her head in alarm and
calls out to alert the herd.

Baring its teeth, the meat-eater chases a helpless little dinosaur. But Baby Duckbill and her family are safe. They stay close together and find shelter deep within the herd.

To escape the danger, a few of the duckbills head for a nearby lake. Mother Duckbill and her babies waddle through the valley with the others. The herd soon settles down again. It's been a long, hard day in the life of Baby Duckbill.

Facts About Baby Duckbill

When Did Duckbill Live?

The duckbilled dinosaur lived during the late Cretaceous Period, about one hundred to sixty-five million years ago. Many different types of duckbills existed, but they all belonged to a group of dinosaurs called the hadrosaurs. The hadrosaurs were harmless and known for their flat bills or beaks, strong tails and webbed or padded fingers. Many of the duck-billed dinosaurs sported boney head crests, some of which were hollow and amplified their bellowing calls to each other. Fossils of one type of duckbill, maiasaura, were first found in 1978 in Montana. They are famous because they contained the first dinosaur nestlings ever found!

What Did Duckbill Eat?

Duckbill was a vegetarian and ate grasses, berries, seeds, shrubs, pine needles and other plants. In the back of its bill were rows and rows of teeth that were perfect for grinding up vegetation. The dinosaur probably stood on its hind legs to reach the treetops and down on all fours to feed on low-growing plants. Fossils suggest that duckbill parents brought food to their babies until they were old enough to forage for themselves.

How Big Was Duckbill?

According to fossils, the hatched maiasaura was a foot long, but grew to thirty feet and weighed up to two tons! When upright, maiasaura stood fifteen feet.

What Was A Duckbill's Family Like?

Fossils show that the maiasauras nested in large colonies, much like today's penguins and gulls do. The round nests were scooped out of the mud and spaced about thirty feet apart (the length of an adult). The fossils also show that the duckbill laid twenty to twenty-five oblong eggs that were about eight inches long, and ridged. The duckbill probably covered its eggs with grasses and reeds and guarded them until they hatched under the warm sun. Some paleontologists (people who study fossils) think that maiasaura protected and cared for its young, unlike most reptiles of today, which desert their eggs. Evidence that the young grew very quickly has led some to believe that the duckbill, like the maiasaura, was warm-blooded. Because the duckbill appears to have been a good parent, Montanan Jack Horner, who discovered the dinosaur, named it Maiasaura, meaning "good mother lizard."

How Did Duckbill Protect Itself?

Duckbill was not equipped with horns, plates or spikes for protection. Nor was the dinosaur built for speed. Yet the duckbill was one of the most numerous and successful types of dinosaurs that lived during the Cretaceous Period. Some paleontologists believed the key to its survival was the fact that it traveled in herds and cared for its young. The dinosaur had keen eyes, ears and noses, and could alarm the herd when in danger of attack. In defense, the duckbill probably disappeared into the forest or jumped into a lake and swam away.

Why Did Duckbill Disappear?

No one knows for sure why the duckbill and the other dinosaurs disappeared about sixty-five million years ago. Most people believe that a huge comet or asteroid crashed into the earth, causing a massive dust cloud that blocked the sun. Without sunlight, plants couldn't live and the air turned very cold. Most dinosaurs couldn't survive the freezing temperatures. Those that could probably died from lack of food. Regardless of how the dinosaurs disappeared, they ruled the earth during the "Age of Reptiles," two hundred to sixty-five million years ago. They thrived for over one hundred thirty million years—longer than any animal has ever lived!